To Abigail,

It's what's inside that matters for everything.

Matthew I Beasley

D1504632

ISBN: 1439231370
ISBN 13: 9781439231371
LCCN: 2009901981

To my very own baby birds
Scotty, Emily, Kimi, Wendy and Nate
and to my P. who makes it all happen

For my kids, Quinn and Tate

About the Author

Matt Beasley is a stay-at-home dad and adoptive father of 5 energetic, amazing, talented and very diverse children. He enjoys reading, writing, coaching soccer, baseball and basketball and helping children learn to read. As a native Californian, Matt spends much of his time on long bike rides and boogie boarding with his kids.

About the Illustrator

Jennifer Hart Morillo currently resides in San Jose, California with her husband, two sons and an wild assortment of critters. Art and all things paper have been some of her passions from an early age. She attended the University of Georgia, graduating with a BFA in 1992 from the Lamar Dodd School of Art. Jennifer's work is often inspired by her love of science and nature.

Cover Design

Special thanks to Andrea Narancic

In front of Mr. Green's old house,
in the big oak tree,
live different kinds of birds in nests.
Look close and you will see.

2

Many kinds of shapes and sizes,
Woodpeckers, Crows and Jays.
All flitting through the bright green leaves
Wonderful like a maze.

3

There is a mama bird you see,
she lives high up in a nest.
She has yellow feathers on her wings,
and brown upon her breast.
In that comfy nest so high
she's got one little son.
A little boy who wishes for
a little bit of fun.

"I want to play with our neighbors,"
said Baby mama's son.
"I'm stuck all day in this nest,
and I'm the only one."

4

"That's the silliest thing I've ever heard.
You can't play with the others.
I don't like our neighbor birds.
I don't like their mothers".

"What's wrong with the other birds, why?"
Baby asked in a voice so high.

5

"Just look at the Crows", mama said,
"they are big and they're black.
Let's face it my son,
its color they lack.
They have drab ugly feathers
from winter to fall.
Big ugly bodies
with no yellow at all."

"They have those big beaks
and they CAW and they PECK.
They make messes with walnuts
they're a pain in the neck."

"And look what they eat,
old hot dogs, apples,
red and green berries.
Even the pits
from Mr. Green's cherries."

"The Blue Jays true,
are as Blue as can be,
but they're big and loud,
surely this you can see?
Their blue is so dark
not light like the sky.
They hop and they shriek
I just wonder why."

8

"Jays eat everything, anything
they can find.
They'll eat lizards and frogs
and bugs of any kind.
They stand there and shriek
atop the old fence.
Really my son it makes no sense."

"The Mockingbirds are so plain in that drab gray and white,
They've got long skinny tails. What a terrible sight.
They sing so loud for goodness sake.
They stand up and sing
on Mr. Green's rake.
They sing, sing, sing, sing,
all night and all day
They steal our songs and scream them
in a horrible way."

"The woodpeckers are up early,
pecking with sharp beaks.
Sometimes all the knocking
gives me headaches for weeks.
Their feet are so big,
so sharp,
and so strong.
It gives me the creeps,
I just think it's wrong."

12

"No, no, you are too young
to leave the nest.
Listen to your mama.
I know what's best."

"But I like the crows," he said.
"They are big and strong.
I like the big beaks."

14

"I love the Mockingbirds song."

15

"The blue of the Blue Jays
is pretty to me.
I like it when the woodpeckers
peck at the tree."

16

"The other birds can be our friends.
I don't see what's wrong.
Every bird has differences,
and sings a different song."

17

"No, no, listen to Mama.
You stay down in the nest.
I'm going off for food now
so lay down and rest."

But Baby did not listen.
He sat and he stared.
He crept to the edge
even though he was scared.

18

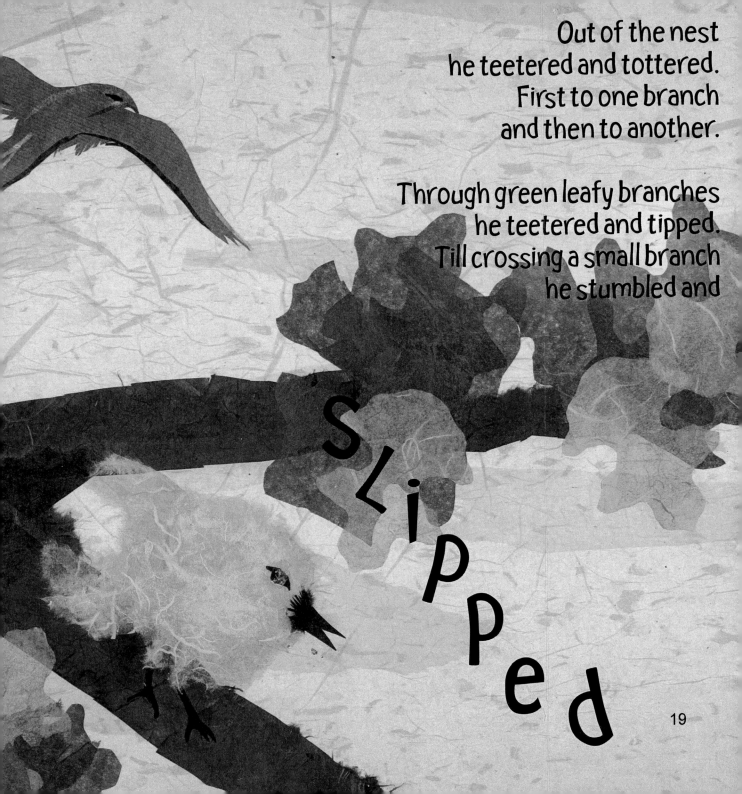

Out of the nest
he teetered and tottered.
First to one branch
and then to another.

Through green leafy branches
he teetered and tipped.
Till crossing a small branch
he stumbled and

SLiPPed

19

DOWn

through the branches
he dropped like a stone.

Past the crows, and the jays,
and the woodpeckers home.

He dropped faster and faster,
and screamed, "Mama come help!"

20

He landed in a big pile of leaves with a "Yelp!"

21

Up on the porch
 the cat opened one eye with a smile.
"Hmm," he said,
"I haven't had fresh baby bird in a while."

22

Baby bird knew of the dangers
on the ground.
So he tried to be still
and not make a sound.
Baby looked around.
He looked far and looked near.
He was starting to think
there was nothing to fear.
He heard a small sound
and turned where he sat.

23

He looked into the eyes
of Mr. Green's cat.

24

Baby couldn't run, or fly up high.
He knew he would end
in the cat's insides.
Baby let out a "peep".
Hoping someone was near.
He cried out louder, "CHEEP",
wishing his mama would hear.

Poor Baby was certain
there was no one around.
Suddenly he heard
An ear splitting sound.

A "CAW CAW" from the Crows.
From the Blue Jays a loud "screeeeeech".
The Mockingbirds sang loudly.
Wild medleys from each.
They swooped down from the tree
and onto the cat.
Pecking and poking
this way and that.

26

Mama returned
and found Baby bird gone.
She heard the commotion,
and knew something was wrong.

28

Mama dove for the ground,
and saw a wonderful sight.
The other birds, her neighbors,
fighting for Baby bird's life.

Something streaked by her
and got to Baby much quicker.
It was the big Woodpecker,
the Red Shafted Flicker.

He grabbed the little bird
in powerful claws
and lifted him skyward
away from the cats deadly paws.

30

He flew to the nest
that was high in the tree.
There he plopped Baby bird,
then flew down to see.
The cat swipe at the birds,
but they were much too quick.
The scaredy-cat ran off
into a hedge that was thick.

31

Up they all flew.
Did they save him in time?
They cheered as they landed,
and saw that Baby was fine.

Up Mama flew
and joined all the rest.
She hopped in and snuggled
Baby bird in the nest.

33

"Oh, my little Baby," she said,
"How could I be so wrong?
We need the strong Crows.
I love the Mockingbirds song.
The Blue of the Jays
is now beautiful to me.
The Woodpeckers can peck.
Now I can see.
You can't judge others
on how they look or sing,
it's what's inside that matters
for everything.
When you are bigger,
you can play with the rest.
Now you can see
Mama knows what's best.

34

Made in the USA
San Bernardino, CA
04 October 2016